Oh My Baby Bear!

For Willa Perlman,
dear friend
and my editor

Requests for permission to make copies of any part of the work should
be mailed to: Permissions Department, Harcourt Brace & Company,
6277 Sea Harbor Drive, Orlando, Florida 32887–6777.

First Voyager Books edition 1995

Library of Congress Cataloging-in-Publication Data
Wood, Audrey.
Oh my baby bear!/Audrey Wood.—1st ed.
p.   cm.
Summary: Baby Bear discovers that he is now old enough
to dress himself, eat breakfast by himself, and give himself a bath,
but perhaps most wonderful of all he will never be too big for a goodnight kiss.
ISBN 0-15-257698-3
ISBN 0-15-200774-1 (pbk.)
[1. Bears—Fiction. 2. Growth—Fiction] I. Title.
PZ7.W846Oh   1990
[E]—dc20   90-7564

B C D E F   A B C D E (pbk.)

Printed in Singapore

The paintings in this book were done in Winsor & Newton
watercolors on Arches watercolor paper.
The display type was set in Windsor Roman and the text type
was set in ITC Garamond Light by Thompson Type, San Diego, California.
Color separations were made by Bright Arts, Ltd., Singapore.
Printed and bound by Tien Wah Press, Singapore
This book was printed with soya-based inks on Leykam recycled
paper, which contains more than 20 percent postconsumer waste
and has a total recycled content of at least 50 percent.
Production supervision by Warren Wallerstein and Diana Ford
Designed by Camilla Filancia

Audrey Wood

Oh My Baby Bear!

Voyager Books

Harcourt Brace & Company

San Diego   New York   London

Every morning when the sun peeped in the window and the birds began to sing, Mama and Papa Bear awakened Baby Bear with a kiss.

They put on his clothes . . .

fed him breakfast . . .

and then sent him outside to play.

In the evening they gave him a bath . . .

and put him to bed. Mama Bear tucked him in, Papa Bear read him a story, and they both kissed him good night.

But one morning Papa Bear said, "We need to hoe our garden. Today you must dress yourself."

Baby Bear tried, but nothing seemed to fit.

"Oh my Baby Bear!" Papa Bear said. "Let me show you how."

When it was time for breakfast Mama Bear said, "Baby Bear, we need to clean our house. Today you must feed yourself."

Baby Bear tried, but what a mess he made!

"Oh my Baby Bear!" Mama Bear said. "Let me show you how."

After breakfast Baby Bear went outside and played
by himself all day long.
"Isn't he wonderful!" Mama and Papa Bear said.

Then Baby Bear went inside to have his bath.
"Tonight we need to bake a pie," Mama Bear said.
"You must bathe yourself."

Baby Bear tried, but soap got in his eyes.

"Oh my Baby Bear!" Papa Bear said. "Let me show you how."

After his bath, Mama and Papa Bear put Baby Bear to bed.

The next morning Baby Bear could hardly wait.

He dressed himself,   ate his breakfast,

played all day long,

and gave himself a bath.

Then, when the moon peeped in the window and all
the birds stopped singing, Baby Bear climbed into bed . . .

and tried to fall asleep.

"Oh my!" Papa Bear cried. "Baby Bear put himself to bed!"
"He's not a baby anymore," Mama Bear said. "From now on
we must call him Little Bear."

"But Little Bears don't have to go to bed so early,"
Papa Bear said. "They can stay up late."
So Little Bear jumped out of bed.

Whistling a happy tune the bears went for a long walk
to see the starry night.

Then they strolled back home and ate some banana-cherry pie.

At last Mama and Papa Bear put Little Bear to bed.

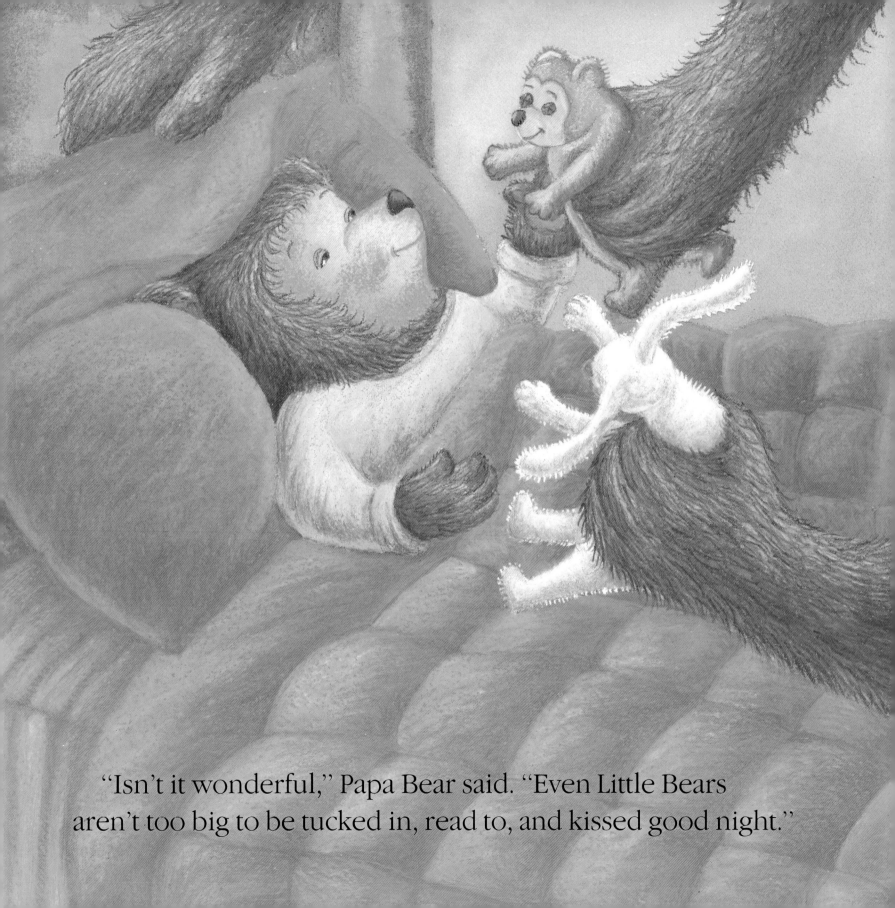

"Isn't it wonderful," Papa Bear said. "Even Little Bears aren't too big to be tucked in, read to, and kissed good night."

But Little Bear didn't hear. He was already asleep,
dreaming Little Bear dreams.